ALL MY FRIENDS

ALSO BY HOPE LARSON

Madeleine L'Engle's
A Wrinkle in Time: The Graphic Novel

Compass South (Four Points Book 1)
Illustrations by Rebecca Mock

Knife's Edge (Four Points Book 2)
Illustrations by Rebecca Mock

All Summer Long (Eagle Rock Series Book 1)

All Together Now (Eagle Rock Series Book 2)

ALL
MY FRIENDS

HOPE LARSON

Farrar Straus Giroux
New York

Farrar Straus Giroux Books for Young Readers
An imprint of Macmillan Publishing Group, LLC
120 Broadway, New York, NY 10271
mackids.com

Our books may be purchased in bulk for promotional, educational, or business use. Please contact your local bookseller or the Macmillan Corporate and Premium Sales Department at (800) 221-7945 ext. 5442 or by email at MacmillanSpecialMarkets@macmillan.com.

Names: Larson, Hope, author, illustrator.
Title: All my friends / Hope Larson.
Description: First edition. | New York : Farrar Straus Giroux Books for Young Readers, 2021. | Series: [Eagle Rock] | Sequel to: All together now. | Audience: Ages 9-14. | Audience: Grades 4-6. | Summary: When Fancy Pink is offered a record deal their parents say no, so they decide to make an album on their own, if they can raise enough money without raising their parents' suspicions.
Identifiers: LCCN 2020052185 | ISBN 9780374311636 (hardcover) ISBN 9780374388669 (trade paperback)
Subjects: LCSH: Graphic novels. | CYAC: Graphic novels. | Musicians—Fiction. | Bands (Music)—Fiction. | Family life—California, Southern—Fiction. | Dating (Social customs)—Fiction. | Racially mixed people—Fiction. | California, Southern—Fiction.
Classification: LCC PZ7.7.L37 Ah 2021 | DDC 741.5/973—dc23
LC record available at https://lccn.loc.gov/2020052185

ISBN 978-0-374-31163-6 (hardcover)
1 3 5 7 9 10 8 6 4 2

ISBN 978-0-374-38866-9 (paperback)
1 3 5 7 9 10 8 6 4 2

Printed in China by Toppan Leefung Printing Ltd., Dongguan City, Guangdong Province
First edition, 2021
Book design by Hope Larson and Molly Johanson
Colored by Hilary Sycamore and Karina Edwards

Electric Guitar
Guitar Strings
10
13
17
26
36
46
NICKEL WOUND
Light
Bronze

March

Echo Park, Los Angeles
Saturday
DA DA DA DA DA DA
dun dun dun

BRAAANG

Bina, 14
Lora, 14
Nok nok
FANCY PINK
Kesi, 13

Turn it down, Kesi!
Mom! You're home early!
BRAAAANG
dun dun dun
Hey, everyone—
BRAAANG
LORA!
Huh?
BRAAANG
BINA!
BINA!
Aaaah!

You need to turn it down. I could hear you all the way at the end of the block.

Really? How'd the bass sound? I just got a vintage distortion pedal, and—

Sorry, Mom. It won't happen again.

Yeah, sorry. We just—we're excited for our show.

Right. When is it, again?

Next week at the Echo! It's, like, a really big deal.

Not that big. We're just the opening band.

Mm. Well. Baby steps.

click

Oooooooof. I **told** you we had to keep it down, but did anyone listen? No!

. . . says the girl playing the loudest instrument.

flop

And anyway, you said she wasn't coming back till six!

Yeah, that's right.

Maybe her last client canceled.

Maybe— maybe she doesn't trust me.

Oh God, what if—

Kesi? Are you spiraling? Is your blood sugar low? I have sour worms!

LARIBO

Ooooh!

One bag of gummies later . . .

Let's end practice early.

I'm not in the mood to keep playing.

munch

rustle

But we haven't practiced the new stuff!

And I'm still deciding which pedal to use!

Playing the Echo's my ultimate dream, and we're **so close** to being ready.

A few more run-throughs and we'll have it locked down. Okay? **Please?**

C'mon, Kes. What do you say?

Well . . .

"Okay."

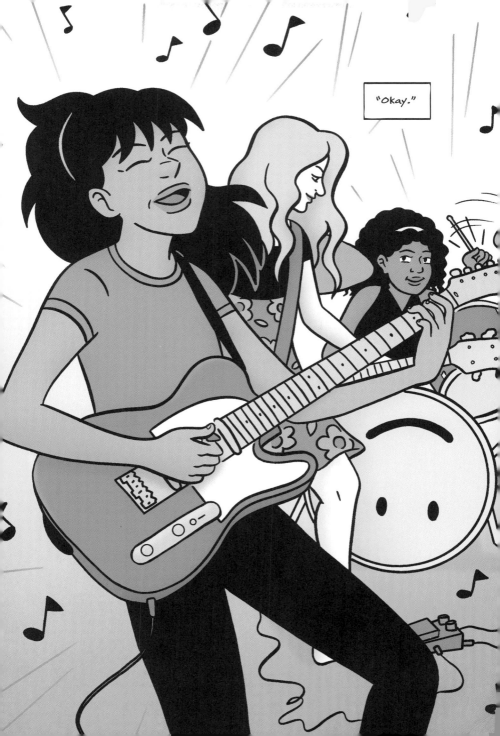

Later

Beep
Beep

How was practice, Bee?

Great, Dad! Thanks for picking me up.

Hungry? Mom's meeting up with her friends, so I was thinking—

BURGERS!

BURGER
—and fries wild style, extra well done.
BURGER
And a Neapolitan shake, please and thank you!
SPLURT
Ahem.
Austin! Hi!
Plain cheeseburger, fries wild style, extra well done, and a Neapolitan shake?
Uh-huh.
Cheeseburger, mustard-grilled patty, hold the tomato?

Yup. Um—I'm here with Charlie. Just needed napkins.

Charlie, Austin's sister

Oh. Cool. I'm here with my dad.

Well, later!

Bye!

Got your ketchup.

Thanks! So, you and Austin are friends again?

Ew, Dad, don't spy on me!

I wasn't. I just—

We're not friends, but we're not NOT friends. Okay? It's complicated.*

*It's complicated.

They were best friends!

Until Austin got a girlfriend and started acting weird.

So Bina made new friends.

Then Austin got dumped, and Bina accidentally went on a kind-of date with him.

awkward

She couldn't figure out if she liked him or not, and ended up dumping him on their first official date.

And now things are weird.

Don't worry. It'll be okay.

I hope so.

11

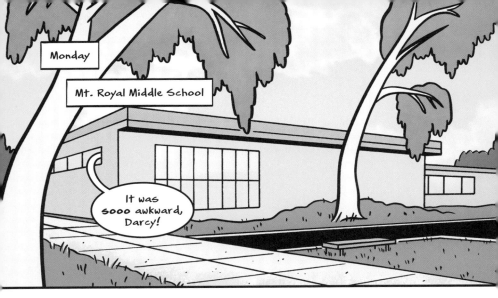

Monday

Mt. Royal Middle School

It was **sooo** awkward, Darcy!

He came over like he wanted to talk, and then it was like he had to get away ASAP.

SLAM

I mean . . . You dumped him on your first date. He's probably not over it yet.

Technically, it wasn't a date.
You're just saying that to make yourself feel better!
Fine! It was a date! It was a date and I messed everything up!
Don't beat yourself up. Just, like, take some responsibility.
Siiigh
I know it's rocky with Austin right now, but maybe it's for the best.
Like, if our band hadn't fallen apart, you wouldn't have met Kesi and Lora and started Fancy Pink.
Yeah . . . I wish they went to school with us, and we could all hang out.

I can't wait for your show!

Opening for Anne Surly is a big deal. Even Enzo's excited.

Uh-huh. Sure he is.

Well, I mean, he **almost** smiled.

He did?! That means a lot!

I know. Don't let us down.

Let you down? I couldn't if I tried!

I was born to play the Echo.

Night of the show
Why don't they let us in already?
I'm gonna cry if Anne Surly doesn't play "Honey Burst." It's my favorite song.
I came here all the time before I had him.
Me too! Memories, right?
Do you know who's opening?
Yeah! This girl from our school, Bina.

"Fancy Pink is her new band."

We're here.

We're at the Echo.

Is this for real? Somebody pinch me.

Ouch!

Thanks.

PINCH

Bitters and soda, please.

You got it.

It's beautiful here, right?

Uh . . .

It's kinda grimy, actually.

You're Lora's dad? Great to meet you! I'm Bina's mom.

DOORS ARE OPEN!

Here we go!

Oh God. I invited my entire friends list. What if they don't come?

What if they **all** come?!

huh

huh

huh

Uh-oh. Bina, did you bring—?

A paper bag? Yep. Here ya go.

huh *huh* *huh* *huh* *uh*

Deep breaths. Yoga breaths.

In—one, two, three. Out—one, two, three.

I'll be Fine—huh—when we're on—huh—stage—

Yeah, you will! We've practiced. We're ready.

We're opening for Freaking **Anne Surly**, and we **earned** it.

I've been waiting all my life to stand on that stage and say—

Hello, Los Angeles!
I'm Bina. That's Lora on bass, and Kesi on drums.

And we're called Fancy Pink.
Still fiddling with her pedals

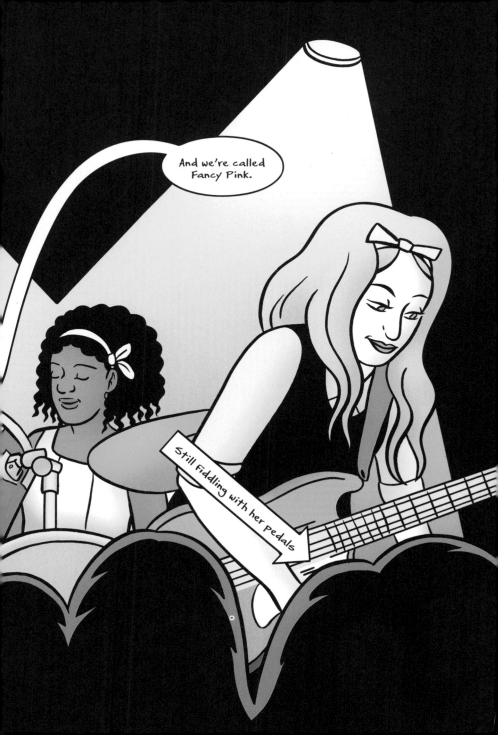

YEEEAH!
Bina's mom
Charlie
Charlie and Austin's mom
Darcy
Enzo
da da da da da
DA DA DA DA DA
DA DA DA DA DA DA DA DA DA DA DA DA DA DA DA
BRAAANG
dun DUN dun dun DUN dun

Jacarandas all in bloom
I got lost in the June Gloom
Skipped ahead and doubled back
Stepped on every single crack
You said you like it complicated
Straight answers are overrated
Well, I've heard that one before
And I'm not listening anymore
Anymore anymore
anymore anymore–
SKREEE
Anymoooooooore
What was that sound?!
Why can't I hear my bass?!

?!
Her distortion pedal's fried!
Distortion
RIP
Noooo! I just got this!
While she switches out her cables, I'll cover her with an
awesome solo!
Wee oooeee AAA—

Wee OOO eeeO
eeAAA—
SNAP!
My string!
OoooOOOOooO

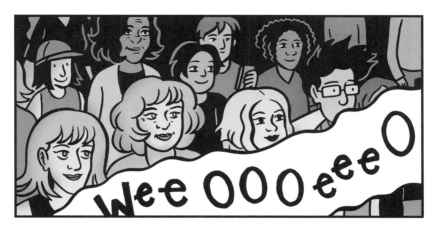

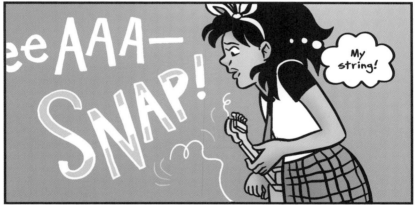

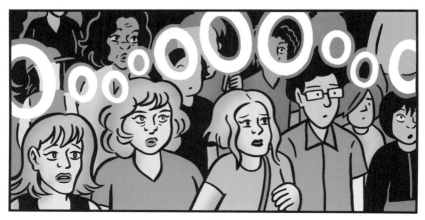

20 minutes later

The green room

Come on. We can't hide in here all night.

Why not? Our set was a literal nightmare.

SNAX for ANNE SORLY =ONLY!!=

Anne Surly's chips

Yeah. Can I have that paper bag back? I think I'm gonna need it.

C'mon. Up! Let's go watch Forbidden Emission. I saw them last month, and they—

—and he takes us to this sick party in NoHo. Some influencer girl's penthouse.

The headliners

and entourage

And her parents are **never** home.

So we're walking around, looking at her stuff, and we end up in this giant closet.

Ooh, really?

Then what?

Everything still has the tags on. It's all stuff these **brands** sent her. So, Noah's like—

Y-you're Cooper! From Anne Surly! We **love** you!

We're Fancy Pink?

We opened for you?

...

Sorry, someone **interrupted.** What was I saying?

"So, Noah's like . . ."

dir

quotes

Right. He's like, "I bet she doesn't even know what she's got in here. We should—"

Take something?!

Leave something.

So he left his crappy old T-shirt full of sweat holes.

And two days later, Influencer Chick was wearing it on Filtergram.

Ha-ha-ha! OMG!

Let's go.

Yeah. It's **stuffy** in here.

They didn't see us play, so there's that, at least . . .

Those snobs! How **dare** they skip our set!

Even if it **was** the worst.

Cooper acts like we're dumb kids, but he's only fifteen!

Really? He seems older.

He's not! My friend goes to his school.

Hey! Fancy Pink! C'mere!

Bring a second guitar next time.

That'll give you a backup if you break another string.

Wow, great tip! I'll head straight out and buy another electric with the zillions of dollars I have lying around.

Aw, I'm just trying to help . . .

Hey! Do you have an EP? I'll check out your stuff.

Um—

Here's a download code.

Thanks! I'll give it a spin.

You don't **have** to, but if you feel like it—

I will. Cross my heart.

KISS ♥

Bye, Bina!

Byyyye!

See you at practice!

Hi.

Oh! There you are, Bee!

Your First big show! I'm so proud of you.

Thanks, Mom . . .

Um, can we skip Anne Surly?

You were so excited to see them. Is everything okay?

Yeah.

I kinda just want to go home.

EXIT

Bina's house

Two weeks later

e-mail ping!

Step

Huh? Who's Steph?

click

Oh!

30

Webmail

Licensing? Inbox ×

StephMerch
to: Fancy Pink
cc: Foster Levin

Dear Bina, Kesi, and Lora,

We met at the Echo. I was doing Anne Surly's merch. I checked out your EP, and it's GREAT. Can I be your #1 fan?

I'm writing because my dad works at Hala (the streaming network), and he's a fan too. He wants to know if you ever license your tracks. Specifically for this show Hala's remaking called *British Teen Private Eye*. If you're interested, he's copied here, and his name is Foster Levin.

(Don't worry, he'll understand if you're too cool to work for The Man.)

Your fan,
Steph

Is . . .
is this for real?
Totally real!
British Teen Private Eye
BTPE
MOOO
OOOM!
Poof

This is like my all-time favorite show. I was **obsessed** with it last summer.
And they're remaking it! And they want to use my band's music!
We can do it, right? If Kesi and Lora say yes?
You mean if their **parents** say yes?
EEEEEE! Thankyouthankyou thankyouthank—
SPROING
And if this company agrees to pay you a fair rate.
I'll talk to Austin's mom—she does this kind of thing for a living.
wobble

Okay . . .

And Bina, your share of any money you get from this deal is going into a trust, for college.

Mom! Dad! This is my big break!

Don't be such killjoys!

Aw, honey. I promise we're excited.

But you're 14! We don't want anyone taking advantage of you.

I know, but **please** don't take this chance away from me. It could change my whole life.

I know, honey.

That's what we're afraid of.

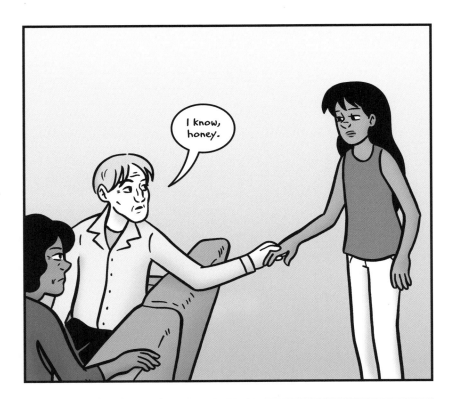

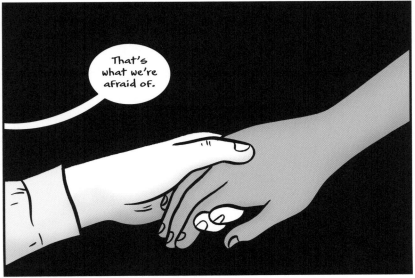

April

One month, 15 e-mails, 275 texts, countless parental misgivings, and a fancy grown-up meeting later . . .

Lora's house

Everybody ready?

They better not have messed with our levels. I mixed them **perfectly**.

They paid us $3,000. I think they're allowed.

Okay, well— here we go!

ZAP

Wooooo!

hala

Seriously, if they changed anything—

Shhh, Lora!

The original was called British Teen Private Eye, but—

L.A. Teen
PRIVATE EYE

We knooow, Bina!

I used to be a normal LA girl. I used to be fun. We totally would've got along.

But when they found a body on the football field, I knew it was up to me to bring **justice** to Dahlia High.

Is that—?

EEEEEEEEEE
You said you like it complicated
Straight answers are overrated
Well, I've heard that one before
And I'm not listening anymore

The next day

That was **so cool**, hearing your music on a show!

Thanks! Wonder if anyone else noticed.

Um, are those sixth graders locker-stalking you?

?

Gasp! That's her! She's so cool!

She's coming over! I'm scared!

Your public awaits.

nudge

Oh God.

What kind of guitar do you play?
Do you take, like, **lessons?**
What does "Fancy Pink" mean?
What's your favorite band?
How did you get your song on **LA Teen Private Eye?**
How much money did they pay you?
When's your next show?
Are you going to go on tour?
Ummmmm, well–

Whew! Fans are intense.
Hey. There she is.
I wonder if people are being weird at Lora and Kesi's schools, too.
Hey. Good job getting your music on that show.
Oh! Thanks.
Here we go again!
Did you know me and Todd have a band?
Cool.
You should jam with us. We could teach you a few things.

"Teach me a few things"?! Ew!

Thanks, but I'm busy with Fancy Pink.

Come on. Me and Todd have been playing music since sixth grade and we can't catch a break. If we had a girl in the band, we definitely would.

Yeah. People give girls way more opportunities. You don't even have to try.

I try. I started learning guitar when I was nine.

Really? Doesn't show at all.

I hope Hala paid you a lot, 'cause you need singing lessons too.

Ignore them, Bina. They're just insecure.

WILL YOU ALL STOP TELLING ME WHAT TO DO?!

Yikes. She scary.

Watch out, Austin.

Sliiiiiink

I was just trying to help.

I know. You were standing up for me, and I—

I'm sorry I yelled at you.

Hey— want to hang out later and catch up?

Yeah, maybe. Come by after school, I guess.

Cool! See you later!

After school

Austin's house

Here goes . . .

GULP

NOK NOK

Hi, Bina.

Hi, Charlie! Is Austin home?

Um, yeah.

So can I come in?

No. He isn't ready to be friends. He sent me out to intercept you.

But he said I should come over.

He said you "put him on the spot" and he "needs time to think."

If it were up to me, I'd lock you both in a room and make you talk things out. But it's not.

Oh.

Okay.

I understand.

Sigh.

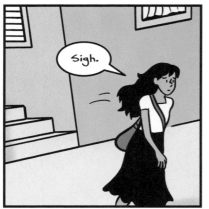

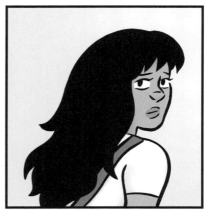

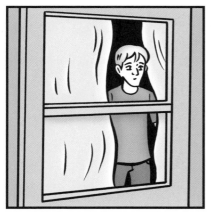

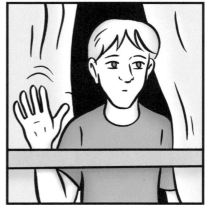

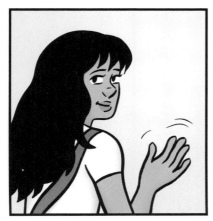

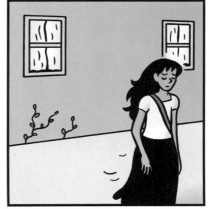

TRADER JOE'S
Later
GROCERY STORE
So, was everyone at school excited about your big debut?
Like four people noticed.
TRADER JOE'S
Two sixth graders acted like I was famous, and two guys in my class were jerks.
You okay?
Yeah. I can take it.
Fine. But if they get any worse, I want you to tell me.
DO do do DO do do DO do
Hello?
Speaking.
Yes, that's my daughter's band.
Who is it?! What do they want?!

Hm.

Mmhm.

Thanks for getting in touch.

END CALL

That was Fourth Room Records. They want to sign Fancy Pink.

FOOM

A label? A label wants to sign us?!

I need to think about this. Talk to your mom, your bandmates' parents . . .

Calm down. Be chill. Impress him with how mature you are.

They "think about" everything. They're going to say yes.

Right. I understand.

This is a big decision. Thanks for taking it in stride.

No problem.

Everything's going according to plan.

The Hollywood Bowl
Fancy Pink
Hello, Los Angeles!
We just got back from our European tour, and we're thrilled to share our homecoming with the city that gave us our start.
Find something to hold on to, 'cause we aren't gonna hold back.
POOF
Bina? Can we come in?
Yeah! Hi!

We've been discussing the whole record label thing.

You have?

Ba DUM Ba DUM

We didn't come to this decision lightly, but . . .

Our answer is no.

What? I . . . I don't understand.

Gigging around town is one thing, but record deals are serious.

This one decision could control your life for years.

You're too young to be caught in the entertainment-industrial complex.

It's not healthy for—well—anyone, but especially not for a teenager.

I don't get it. You tell me I can do anything, but when I get the chance, you ruin everything.

It's not just **our** decision, Bee.

Kesi's and Lora's parents feel the same.

Please leave.

GO AWAY!!!

I know you're disappointed, but—

SCREEEAAM
So much for acting mature.

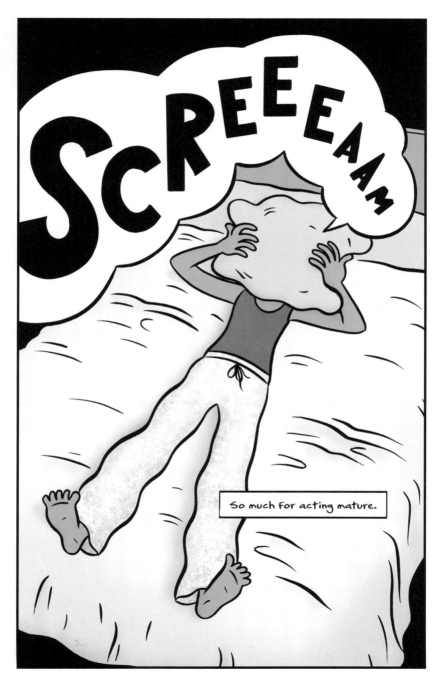

Echo Park, Los Angeles

Saturday

Our parents are being such jerks!

I'm glad it's not just mine who're being strict.

I yelled at mine. They made me write an apology letter before I left the house.

We were about to go next level, and they just took it away.

Why don't they get what a big deal this is?

'Cause they're old.

I'm getting a refill.

Bina! Get me another croissant. I'll pay you back!

Okay—

Watch it!

Oops! Sorry!

No big. Saved by my feline reflexes.

Hey. Don't I know you?

!!

Yeah. From the Echo greenroom.

You were mean to my band. Remember?

Oh crap. You're, uh . . .

Fancy Nancy?

Fancy Pink. Remember it. You'll be seeing a lot of us.

Later
Kesi's house
"Don't I know you?"
What a jerk.
RAT-TA-TAT

He can go ahead and underestimate us.
If he's not paying attention, it'll be that much easier to take him down.
I wish he wasn't cute, though. It's such a **waste**.

He has good style, but he's only, like, medium-cute.
BZZT BZZT

Um.
Whoa.
What?
Speak of the devil and he shall text.
???
Hey, Steph (merch) sent me your tracks. They're great. Sorry we got off on the wrong foot.
Anyway, Anne Surly is recording an EP at Red Cent Studios and your voice is perfect for a guest vocal. Interested?
(This is Cooper from the coffee shop.)
Text Message
That's not an apology! He's not taking responsibility.
Yeah. Gross.
But it's a cool opportunity. You should do it.

I don't know. One, he's a jerk.

Two, I don't think my parents would let me.

So? Don't tell them. We'll cover for you!

Why are you so desperate for me to do this?

'Cause you'll get to learn how recording works.

The only thing really stopping us from recording our own album is, we don't know how.

Yeah! Who needs a record label? Who needs parental permission?

"No, Kesi."
"Turn it down, Kesi."
I'm over it!

Let's make a record ourselves!

So, Bee, what do you think?

Okay. I'll tell him I'm in.

How was practice?
Fine.

We're making a record. It'll be awesome. Too bad I can't tell you about it.

Uh, Dad? Mom? What are you listening to?
tick-tock
$
tick-tock

Oh, this? It's Kesha. A guilty pleasure of mine.
Is she the one who sued her manager for multiple kinds of assault?
tick-tock
Mmhm. Her producer. The same guy who convinced her to drop out of high school and make a record with him.
Cool. I get it. This is a teachable moment.
Uh. Well, anyway . . . Anything noteworthy happen today, Bina?
Nope.
I take it back. I don't feel bad for lying. What's the point of having a conversation?
They can't see the world in shades of gray. They think everything's black and white.

Next Saturday

Highland Park, Los Angeles

Enjoy the movie, honey! I'll be back at four to pick you up.

Okay.

Later, Ms. Loop!

Bye!

VROOM!

Do you think your parents suspect . . . ?

No, but I mean, we're barely talking right now.

There's a good taco truck around here.

No time for tacos, Lora! Come on. The studio's this way.

This is so exciting! Do you feel ready?

Yeah, mostly! I've been practicing with the demo Cooper sent me.

Red Cent Studios

You're sure this is it? What if he's messing with us?

It's the address he gave me.

Bina!

. . . and entourage.

You remember my bandmates, Lora and Kesi.

Of course!*

*Nope.

It's a tight space, and the engineer's kinda touchy, but, hey . . .

The more the merrier.
GASP!
Look at all this gear!
It's like a spaceship in there!
GLARE
DO NOT TOUCH THE GLASS.
Eep!

Dakota, this is Bina, the guest vocalist.

Is this your studio?

YES.

It's amazing!

Does he have to yell at us?

If I wasn't in a band, I'd wanna be a sound engineer.

WE'LL RECORD YOU IN THE SMALL BOOTH.

This is the big booth?

GO BACK OUT TO THE HALLWAY.

TAKE THE DOOR ON YOUR LEFT.

I'LL MEET YOU.

The small booth

A bathroom?!

Are you pranking me, Cooper?

No, seriously, the sound in here is incredible.

Put these on. Need lyrics?

Nuh-uh. Got them memorized.

See? She's a pro.

Give the mic space. She's not cheap stage gear. You gotta romance her.

Okay!

EVERYONE OUT!

Bina? Can you hear me?

Dakota! Yes! Hi!

If you're ready, we'll take it from the top.

gulp

Ready!

Okay.

We're rolling.

Ooooh Oooooh
I wanna be sincere but it's so much easier to be clever
When you say that you and me that you and me will last forever
Ooooh Forever
Ooooh Oooooh
Don't believe in forever
Nice. One more take, then we'll go back and double the "oooh's."
Ready when you are.

An hour later

You killed it in there! Thanks for doing this.

Thanks for inviting me.

You're not such a jerk after all.

Not always.

I'll text when we've got a mix!

Can't wait to hear it!

Ummm, that was . . .

AMAZING!

Like, how they recorded you in the bathroom?

So punk rock!

Right?!

It's official. We can for sure make a record.

All we do is show up, and the engineer makes us sound good. Easy!

We should start thinking of names for our label! How about—

Hold up. How much will all this cost?

The practical one

Oh . . .

No clue.

I could ask Cooper what he's spending.

His band has a record deal, though. They aren't the ones paying.

What about—

Bina, doesn't your friend's mom work with bands?

Yeah, Austin's mom. But she might tell my parents, so that's out.

Okay, then . . . Remember Fred from GBGB? Let's ask him.

Ugh. No. He'll want to be involved, or take credit, or—

Wait! I know someone! It's a long shot, but . . .

BANK HOLIDAY

NOW SHOW...

Ooooh, who is it?

Um, Bee? Your mom's waving to us.

Highland

Eek! We're back just in time.

How was Bank Holiday?
Oh— the movie. Fine.
CENTER
TIRE
Should Dad and I go see it?
If you want.
What's wrong, Bina?
Nothing.
I know you're upset about the record deal, but it's not nice of you to treat me like this.

What?! What am I doing?!

One-word replies, evasive answers— I'm not stupid! You're shutting me out.

Whatever.

SCRECH

I'm not a monster, and I'm not your chauffeur.

You're a good kid, and you haven't heard a lot of no's because, so far, you haven't needed to.

Maybe I could've done a better job teaching you to handle disappointment, but your behavior right now isn't on me. It's on you.

Sorry.*

*Not sorry.

SLAM

Sigh
CLICK
Steep Streets
TRACKS
Last summer
You gotta start a band!
I will, when I'm good enough!
Gaia, frontwoman of Steep Streets
Standing-in-front-and-singing-all-the-lyrics superfan
steepstreetsband@g
CLICK

Dear Gaia,

You won't remember me, but I was at your LA show. You gave me your record and told me to start a band.

I don't have a turntable yet, but I did start a band. Actually, two bands, since the first one didn't work out. The second one did, but we need some help.

A label wanted to sign us, but our parents said we're too young, so we decided to make a record ourselves. We aren't sure how to start, though, or how much it will cost. (Eeeeek.)

I know you're really busy, but if you have any advice, please write me back.

Your fan,
Bina Loop

Somewhere in Oakland, CA
Nguyen! I'm going on break!
Menu
ding
band.
n't work
e help.
Hi Bina!
Glad you started a band. Love that you're sticking it to The Man. I'm happy to help you DIY your album.
First, the bad news: recording and mastering aren't cheap. If you're doing it in a studio, not on a laptop in your bedroom, the least you can realistically spend is—

Tuesday afternoon

Kesi's house

$2,500.

And that's if we do it cheap and call in favors.

We're never going to raise that much! I'm not even allowed to get a job till next year.

I have some money saved, but my mom monitors my checking account.

If I take anything out, she'll know.

I babysit, but I'd need years to save up.

What's annoying is we'd have enough if our parents let us use the money from *LA Teen Private Eye*.

My big sister might loan us something.

I'm an only. But don't you have brothers, Bina? Can they help?

Hmm. My brother Johnny lives in Berkeley and has a husband and a cute baby and he makes bank.

He might loan us something.

I can't just call him and ask for two thousand dollars . . .

But I've got a plan.

Silence

chew chew · Slurp

Mom, Dad—

She speaks!

Um, spring break is soon, and I was wondering—

Here we go. What now?

I haven't even asked yet!

You're right. I'm sorry. What is it?

Bina's Plan, Step One: Go to Berkeley

Can I go to Berkeley and visit Johnny?

Dad and I have to work.

I've flown by myself before. I want to see Johnny and Deon and the baby.

I miss them. I want to be a good aunt.

That's not a bad idea!

Hm.

Things have been tense around here. We could all stand to take a break and hit the reset button.

So, can I go?

Please?

—and while I'm there, I'll get him to loan me some money,* and then Fancy Pink can make an album!

*Not sure how, but that's a problem for Future Bina.

You're unstoppable. I've never met a girl as ambitious as me.

Go on.

You sound great on the new song. Did I tell you we finished the mix?

When can I hear it?!

Well, I was thinking, we could get ice cream and I'd play it for you, and we'd, um . . .

Get to know each other.

Wait.

Stop.

Is this, like, a date?

Do you want it to be?

Is it?

• • •

Oh, man—this was a mistake. You're not interested. Pretend I never opened my big dumb—

COOPER! Stop!

Let's go on a date.

Wait. Really?

Yeah. But no pressure, right? If it doesn't work out, we can still be friends?

Definitely. I promise.

No pressure at all.

plink
plink
plink
Bina?
Uh-huh?
Dinner in ten.
Okay.
Um—can I please get ice cream with my friend after school on Friday?
We want to try the new place on Colorado. I can walk there from school.
Sure, honey.
Ugh. I hate this. I'm lying about everything.

Mom, wait—

It's a guy. My friend. He asked me on a date. Can I still go?

Oh.

How old is he?

Um . . . Fifteen.

My band opened for his band.

Thanks for being honest with me.

Aaand that's a no.

You can go. For one hour.

But I'll be working at the coffee shop next door, and you'll come meet me right after.

No way! I can't believe it!

Thanks, Mom! You're the best.

The date

softboy SOFT SERVE

Cof

OPEN

This feels so different from my "date" with Austin.

Thanks.

Uh-huh.

There isn't so much pressure. We haven't been friends for years. We barely know each other.

When do you leave for SF?

Berkeley. I'm going up tomorrow afternoon.

Cool.

awkward SILENCE

Do you always date girls in bands?

I always wanted to date a cool music girl. But you're the first one.

He thinks I'm cool!

Maybe you'd have had better luck if you weren't so mean to us.

nyah!

Probably!

But I'm not interested in anyone who isn't, like, on my level.

Ohhhhh, so most girls aren't "on your level"?

Most **people** aren't on my level.

You're so full of yourself!

Takes one to know one!

Fair. But you have to be a **little** self-obsessed so you don't give up. Right?

As a musician, I mean.

Did . . . did I say something wrong?

Sorry—I was listening. I like this band.

SCRITCH

Oh, Swearin'? Me too! This place has good music.

Did you know Allison Crutchfield lives around here?

Yeah! I follow her on Filtergram. I wish we were friends.

If you like her, you're going to love—

blah blah blah blah blah blah blah blah blah blah blah blah blah blah blah bl blah

87

The next day

Los Angeles International Airport

Safe travels, cool music girl.

Weird. I might actually like him.

88

At least, I like that he likes me.

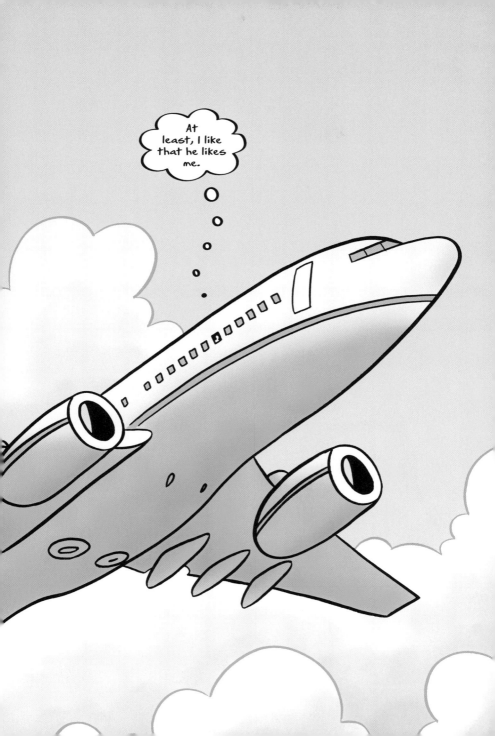

Johnny!
Bina!
Thanks for picking me up!
I wasn't about to tell my kid sister to get on the BART.
I'm so glad I'm here. I needed a break from Mom and Dad.
Mom said things have been tense at home.
Yeah . . .
Long story.
Let's get food and talk it out. I know a great place.
TAXI
TAXI

We'll have the latkes and two pastrami sandwiches.

And an apricot hamantaschen to go.

You got it.

SAUL'S
DELICATESSEN
1966
BREAKFAST - LUNCH - DINNER

Mmm. Celery soda is good.

So, what's the drama at home?

Ugh, well, my band got offered a record deal, but all of our parents said no.

We're too young and vulnerable, supposedly.

They're just trying to keep you safe.

Too safe. Sheltered.

Maybe. My perspective on that stuff changed when I became a parent.

Bina's Plan, Step Two: Ask For $$$

Oh.

Argh! I should've thought this through.

There's no way he'll lend me the money.

You're more of a rebel than I was at your age. I was always afraid to get in trouble.

Unless . . .

Do you ever wish you had?

Yeah. Sometimes.

Does that mean you'd help me get in trouble?

What exactly do you have in mind?

Johnny and Deon's condo

—so, to record our album in a studio, we need to raise about $2,500.

That's a lot of money to us, but I'm sure that to you—

It's a lot to us, too. Nice try, though.

Hm. But maybe . . .

matching funds?

That's a thought.

What are matching funds?

Da!

You raise half the budget on your own—so, about $1,250.

Once you've done that, we match that amount.

We don't put our money on the line until you've done some hard work on your end.

$1,250.

Twelve hundred and fifty dollars.

WAAAAH!

Yeah, I feel the same way.

Uh-huh.

WAA'

WAAAAH!

You're a hustler. You'll find a way.

The next day

Sightseeing in SF

How, though? Twelve hundred dollars is huge.

San Francisco Museum of Modern Art

So we'll start here, check out the Richard Serra, then head to the aquarium.

And tomorrow, rent bikes and ride across the Golden Gate.

Cool!

SF MO MA

Or, if we're too tired to bike tomorrow, we can pick something else.

I got prepaid passes with lots of options.

Can I see the list?

Here you go.

Prepaid passes...

Yeah, they're great. You pay in advance and they give you a nice discount.

SCROLL
SCROLL

CLANK

GRIND

ding

Here! Let's ride bikes, I guess.

Cool.

Wait—

Plink!

TIPS

Shouldn't you save your pennies for your record?

It's okay. I don't mind sharing.

'Cause I know how I'm going to get the money for my band!

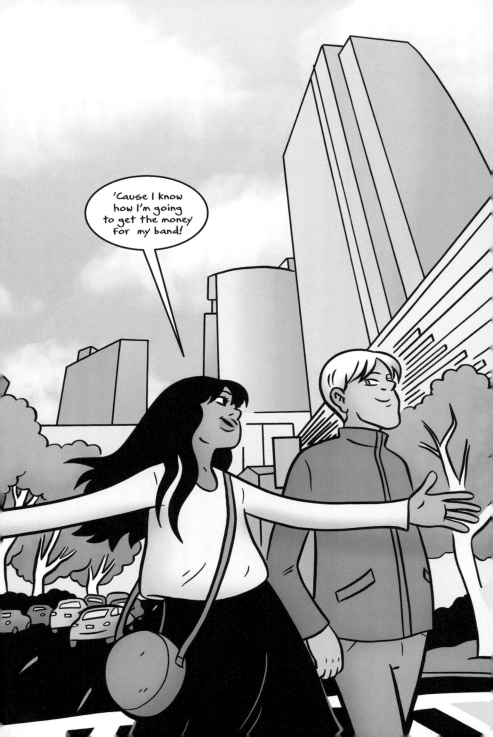

THE UNITE
ONE

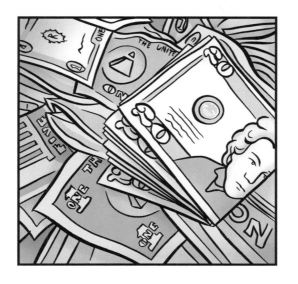

May

Hi, Regina! How are you?
I'm calling to confirm that I'm babysitting Henry this Sunday.
Yes? Great!
If you have a minute, there's something else I want to ask.
Would you be interested in buying a block of babysitting time to help me fundraise for an art project?
You'd pay in advance, but you'd get a special discounted rate.
KICK
The project? It's my band. We want to make a record.
twiddle

Really?! Thank you so much! I really appreciate your support.
Okay. See you Sunday. Bye, Regina.
Score!
Prepaid Babysitting
Shana: $120
Tom: $150
Regina: $20
That makes . . . $470. Not bad at all!
When Kesi and Lora throw in their shares, it's matching funds, here we come!

Friday afternoon

Lora's house

First order of business: Fundraising!

How much have y'all got?

Ahem—

You know how sometimes you put on an old coat, and you check the pockets, and—

How about you, Lora? Did you score big digging through couch cushions?

Twenty bucks. Wow.

I did okay, actually! My sister loaned us a hundo, and I sold some clothes online.

$235!

We're up to $725, which means Johnny will match the funds when we raise another, uh . . .

Shff Shff Shff

$525.

How'd you do that so fast?

Drumming is math. Math is drumming.

We could raise $500 if we crowdsourced online.

Nope. No internet. My parents have Google Alerts for Fancy Pink.

Y'all, it's okay.

"It's okay"? How come you're so chill? It's not like you.

I've been running worst-case scenarios for weeks—thank you, anxiety—and I have a backup plan.

You do?

Two words.

Benefit.

Show.

FOOM FOOM

We'll play, we'll get our friends to play, and we'll put the money from the door toward our album.

I bet Darcy and Enzo would be down.

And Anne Surly **has** to play, right? Since you're dating Cooper?

They'll bring a crowd for sure!

Um— I'll ask him.

Awww, she's blushing!

You liiiiike him!

I . . . I do. We have lots in common, and I kinda tricked him into thinking I'm cool.

I wanna date a cute band guy. Hey, is Anne Surly's drummer single?

Ignore her, Bina. When are you seeing Cooper again?

Cooper! Hey!
Hey, stranger.
TAP
TAP
TAP
TAP
Sorry I haven't texted. I'm babysitting every waking moment, raising money for the album.
How's that going?
TAP
TAP
TAP
TAP
Actually, we're planning this benefit show. Do you think Anne Surly could play?
TAP
TAP
Definitely!
Yesss!
fist pump
Where/when?
TAP
TAP
Still working on that.
TAP
Also wondering if you want to hang out again.
TAP
TAP
TAP

Saturday?
Ooh, a weekend date?
TAP
TAP
My friend's band, Buy Generic, is playing the Hi Hat. Know them? You'd like them.
I'll ask the wardens.
TAP
TAP
TAP
Wait . . .
They won't let me go without a chaperone. Not at night.
TAP
TAP
TAP
My dad's coming. Does that help?
Also, parents LOVE me. ;)
Good. I'm counting on it.
TAP
TAP

Saturday evening
Moooooom! They're here!
nok nok
Hi!
You must be Cooper. And you're . . .
Jason, Cooper's dad.
Isobel.
Those are lovely flowers, Cooper.

They're to thank you for letting Bina come with us.

What a lovely gesture!

Look out for this one, Jason. She can be trouble.

Mom!

No problem. Got my peepers lasered last year.

Ready, kids?

Yes, sir.

Yeah!

Be good!

Okaaaay!

HIGHLAND PARK
BILLIARDS
BEER + WINE
MEXICAN FOOD
5098
THE
HI HAT
LIVE
MUSIC
Do you go to lots of shows together?
Yep. Ever since Cooper was little.

You grew up in the music scene! You're so lucky.
Def made it easier to get noticed when I started Anne Surly. Everyone knew me already.
Cooooooooooper!
Hey!
Who's this? Introduce me!
Bina, this is Prue. She writes this great zine, **Pruberty**.
Cool. I'll check it out.
What's your deal, Bina? I've never seen you around.
I'm around. I'm in a band. Fancy Pink.
She just did guest vocals on our record.

I like her better than the last one.

"The last one"?

Come on. She was nice, just . . .

Just boring.

What are you listening to, Bina?

This feels like a test.

Um, I'm obsessed with AC/DARCY's new digital EP.

Just reviewed it for the zine. It slaps.

Definitely a test.

It does, but I'm biased. I was in a band with Darcy and Enzo.

Interesting.

Oh! Is that—?

Wait. Are you the girl who broke up their show and—

'Scuse me! I see someone I need to talk to.

Fred! Hey!

Huh? Oh, Bina!

Fred, booker/promoter at all-ages DIY space GBGB

Sup, girl? Excited for Buy Generic?

I don't really know them. I came with Cooper.

Hold up. The Frontwoman of Fancy Pink and the Frontman of Anne Surly . . . ?

Anything within my power.

Calm down. It's only our second date.

Anyway.

I was hoping you could do me a giant favor.

So, Kesi and Lora and I are doing a benefit show to cover our recording costs—

Rad! I'll be there.

Aaactually, I was hoping you'd give us the room at GBGB for, like . . . free?

Oh . . .

Er . . .

No? Okay. I know it's a lot to ask.

It's not that . . .

What?! But why?

There's no more GBGB. The city shut us down.

There was a Fire at a warehouse party up in Oakland. Total nightmare. People **died.**

The city doesn't want the same thing happening here, so they're shutting down alternative spaces, and GBGB got caught in the net.

That sucks, Fred. I'm sorry.

I'll Find another spot, but for now . . .

Sorry I can't help.

It's okay. I know you would if you could.

Lemme know where you land! I'll help get the word out.

I will! Thanks, Fred!

He's still playing that knockoff Strat? Lame.

Yep. Amateur hour.

Lots of pro musicians play cheap guitars.

Uh, maybe for endorsement money—

Hey, did you hear GBGB got shut down?

Oh. Too bad.

Another Fred Failure™.

Ever hear his band? Painful—and not in a cool way.

ha na HA HA ho HA HA HA HA HA HA ha ha HA ho

Those who can't play, promote.

I know he's weird, but he's helped me out a lot. AC/DARCY, too.
He really cares about music.
He just wants an excuse to hang with us real musicians.
And journalists.
Yeah. We're the ones who make the scene.
And everyone else should, what, keep away from us?
They should maintain a respectful distance.
GLARE
Eep!
ANNE SURLY
I don't see why you all take everything so seriously.
pat pat
Aw, Bina. You're so pure.
Don't worry. We'll toughen you up.

Why do I have to toughen up?
Why can't they just be nice?
SIGH.

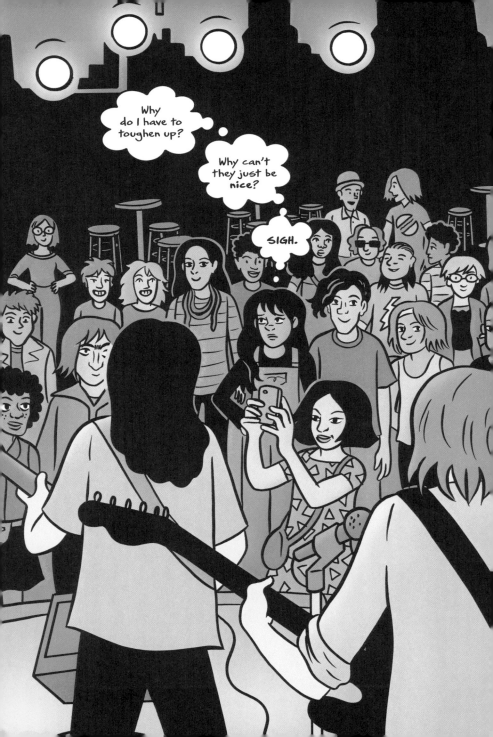

Later
shuff
shuff
shuff

Thanks for coming tonight. I had a good–
I think we should just be friends!

Sorry. I had to get it out.

It's okay.

Really?

I wasn't feeling the chemistry either.

Phew. The music scene's just so small, and I don't want things to be awkward, and—

Oh! Will you still play Fancy Pink's benefit?

Of course! You're going places.

I'd be stupid not to come along.

Let's hang out soon. As friends.

Compatriots in music.

Yeah. Definitely.

I'm home!

Have fun?

It was all right.

I like him! He knows how to make a good impression.

Yeah . . .

We decided to just be friends.

shrug

Do you want to talk about—?

No!

Good night.

SHUT

Good night . . .

Monday

So you're done with Cooper?

Romantically? Yeah. He's cool, but his friends are jerks, and when he's around them, so is he.

I don't want to date someone who thinks I need to "toughen up."

I wanna date someone who likes who I am **now**.

Yeah. You should date someone who thinks you're perfect.

But I'm **not** perfect.

I want someone to see me and **get** me, and—

Plain cheeseburger, fries wild style, extra well done, and a Neapolitan shake?

122

SNAP

Bina? Where'd you go?

Burgers.

Uh, I mean, I'm just worried about finding a space for the benefit.

Enzo and I played the Sinkhole in Cypress Park, and that might work.

It's a big old house, and they do shows in the basement.

Want me to text them?

That would rule!

Okay.

—Fries wild style, extra well done, and—

Sent!

TAP
TAP
TAP
TAP
TAP
TAP
TAP

Sure you're okay?

Yeah! Don't worry.

"Everything's Fine."

CLUNK CLUNK

Oof.

Austin gets me. And I get him.

Mustard-grilled patties are gross, but I like that he orders them that way.

And it's not just burger orders—it's everything. Why didn't I realize how special that is?

POOF!
Snap out of it, Bina!
We had our chance to date Austin and we blew it.
POOF!
Can't we change our mind? We needed time to think!
Oh, really? 'Cause we tried that before and it didn't help!
Ugh! Shut up!
POP
POP
I didn't say anything!
Eep!
Sorry!

RUMMAGE
PLOP
RUSTLE
Hey, Bina—
Austin! Wh-what's up?
BA-DUM BA-DUM
You dropped your pencil case.
Oh. Thanks!
No prob. See you later.
Bye!

That wasn't too weird.

Standing next to him didn't make me feel, like, **crazed** or anything.

I like him, I like him not. I like him, I like him not. I like him—

Um? You're in my seat?

Wha?

Aren't you in, like, eighth grade?

Huh?

BRIIIIIIING
Sixth-grade humanities
Oops.
I'm in the wrong room.
I'm in the wrong year.

What's wrong with me?! How'd I get so turned around?
POOF
Don't pretend like we don't know.
POOF
Yep. It's settled. We **definitely** like him.

So, it's official. I'm crushing on Austin.

But why would he give me another chance?

He's got no reason to trust me.

I wish I could make him feel what I'm feeling.

Maybe I can.

BZZT
BZZT
Unknown
BZZT
Unknown
mobile
Remind Me
Message
Hello?
Ohmygosh! Really?! They'll be so excited!

Kesi's house

It's cool we're getting a room for free, Bina, but I wish we didn't have to do a daytime show.

RAT-A-TAT

FANCY PINK

Are you kidding? A daytime Saturday show is perfect!

street fruit salad

One, our parents won't suspect anything.

TA TAT TA TAT TA

Two, our friends with curfews will get to come.

TAT TA TA TAT TA TAT

Three, would you **please** stop drumming?! You're making me anxious!

Sorry!

Ahem—

How's this look?

Anne Surly
AC/DARCY
Secret Headliner
Help [REDACTED] raise $ to record their first album!
Benefit Show
Saturday, June 1, at 3 p.m.
The Sinkhole
Cypress Park
$10 at the door
Who can resist a secret show, right?
Our friends will know it's us, our **parents** won't—
and a few randos might come to see if the headliner's somebody famous.

vrt vrt vrt vrt vrt vrt vrt

Ready?
Ready!
COPIES
NOTARY

Rrrrrrrrr

RESH
POST
BILL

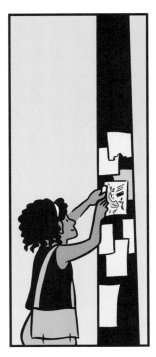

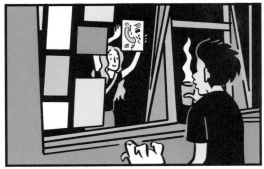

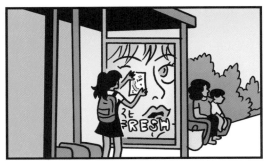

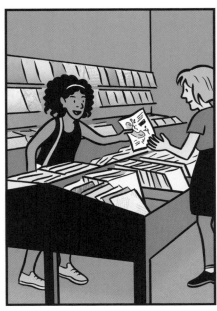

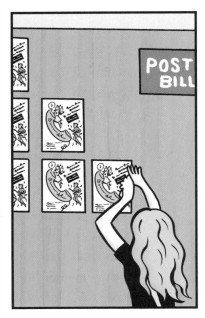

SOCCER
TRYOUTS!
VOLUNT
WITH
Catlan
cat shel
415.
That's Austin.
415
Scribble
See you there?
Pretty please,
mustard-grilled,
hold the tomato?
P.S.
The secret
headliner is
me!

fold

fold

415

I hope he comes.

But even if he doesn't, the show's gonna be amazing.

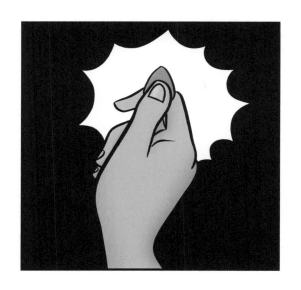

June

Day of the show

GASSSSP

What if it's not amazing?!

What if it's like our show at the Echo?

Are you okay, Bee? You don't look well.

Maybe you shouldn't go to Kesi's this afternoon.

NO! I'm Fine!

I stayed up too late. That's all.

If you're sure—

I am!

I'm just nervous.

I'll Feel better if I practice.

SNAP!
Oh God.
Oh no.
This is
a sign.

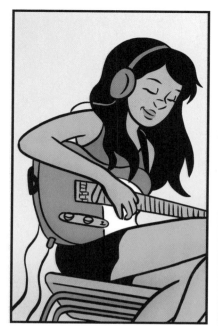

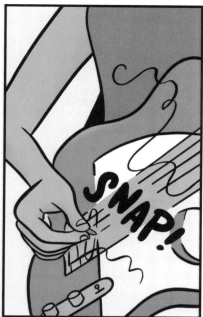

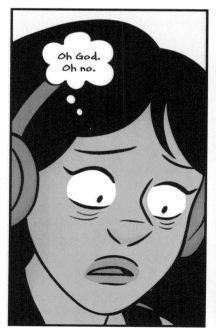

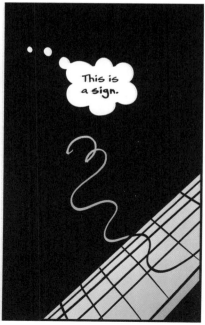

It's going to be a disaster!

I'm going to humiliate myself **again!**

I'm going to—

Bina! Shut up!

Just 'cause things went wrong before, it doesn't mean they will again.

PAT PAT

Sniff

I bet every one of your favorite rock stars has broken, like, a million strings.

SLUMP

Yeah . . . But they have roadies to hand them another guitar.

142

Roadies?! Come on! Keep it in perspective: You're playing a basement, not a stadium.

Thanks, Charlie. That makes me feel better.

It's scary, but you can do this. I promise.

POKE

Great!

See you tonight.

Charlie?

Ya?

Is Austin coming? I put a flyer in his locker, but . . .

Um . . . I don't think so.

Oh.

I don't know if you can change his mind, but I wrote a new song.

For him.

I wrote a song for him.

No promises, okay? But I'll do my best.

Cypress Park, Los Angeles
The Sinkhole
I heard the headliner's a **big deal** and they're testing new material.
Nah. It's Fancy Pink. They're not big yet—
but they **will** be.
Is that them running the door?
ROCK SHOW
Fred! Thanks for coming!
No prob. I spread the word, too.
What's the cover? Ten?
Yeah, but you're totally free to donate more.

Hey. Bina.
Uh-huh?
Come tiebreak our set list.
Be right back!
Okay!
So, options.
"Airplane" is a crowd-pleaser.
"Streaming" slays, but it's new and we're still working out the kinks.
GREEN ROOM

Take a risk. Play "Streaming."
Ugh.
That's what Enzo said . . .
OMG. Did Enzo and I just agree on something?!
Yeah!
Whoa.
Hey, Enzo! Thanks for bringing your kit!

Sniff
Hey—what's wrong?
GREEN ROOM
It's just a lot, you know?
Everyone's working so hard to make this show happen.
Everyone's being so nice.
Um, not everyone.
Your ex just walked in with some girl.
He wasn't my boyfriend, so he's not, like, my ex, but . . .
Really?!
Oh—that's just Steph. She does Anne Surly's merch.

I kinda doubt that's all she does.

Aw, there's no way!

I sent him my new song last night, and we texted for an hour, but he never mentioned—

I know you're friends, but it's lame that he didn't warn you.

Are you sure you're okay?

Uh . . .

I . . .

AHEM.

What's happening here?

flinch

Me and Steph? Yeah. It was, um, unexpected.

You're not upset, right? 'Cause you broke things off, so . . .

It's cool, Cooper. She's cool. I approve.

Thanks.

We're getting food after the show, and you should come if you're not—

Bina!

Charlie!

And Mystery Girl!

This place is, like, so real.

I know, right?

I'm excited. Plus, no pressure, but this is Mia's first show ever.

squeeze

First ever?! Eek! I hope you have fun!

I already am.

Jeez. Has everyone else found love?!

Um, so . . . Where's Austin?

Um, he's just—
Just not ready!
I get it!
It's okay!
STOPPP!
Bina—
It's okay!
WOOSH
Stupid, stupid, stupid.
CLC
CLOMP
CLOMP
OMP
GASP!

AUSTIN!

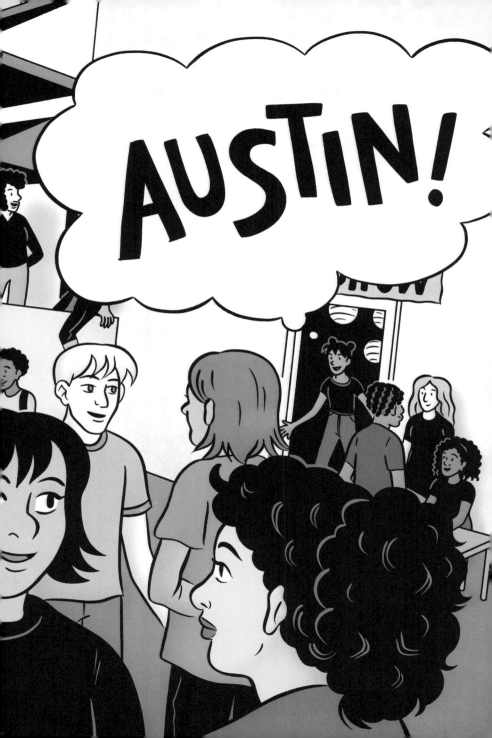

He came.
Oh yeah?! Awesome!
But . . . What if my plan doesn't work?
Ummm, you'll probably write a song about being heartbroken.
And we'll put it on the EP, and everything will be okay, and—
URP?
Eww, Lora. Are you okay?
Yeah, sorry! I had street tacos on the way over.
STIIINK
You sure? That belch was **rank.**
SSSSTIIINK
Um—

Hey.

Hey! Thanks for coming out!

Charlie said I should, so...

SHRUG

See you in there.

URP!

Yup!

Uh-huh!

$10

Oh God. Did you hear him?!

He only came 'cause Charlie made him!

Hey, at least we got his money.

Ugh.

HEY!

AC/DARCY'S STARTING!

BOM
DAT DA
DA
bom
bom
BOM
DAT

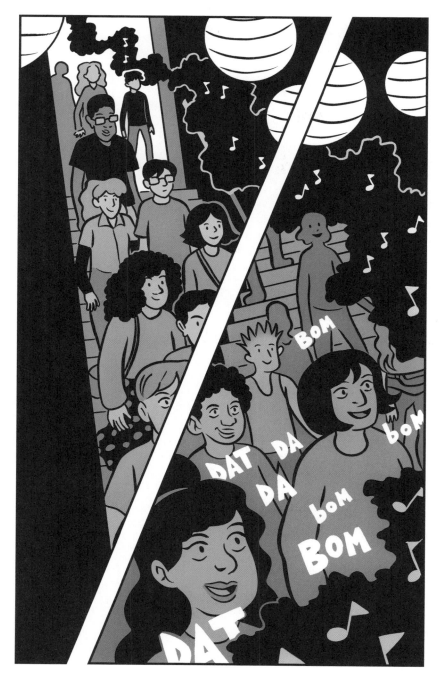

AC/DARCY
BOM
bom
bom
DA
DAT
DAT
DAT

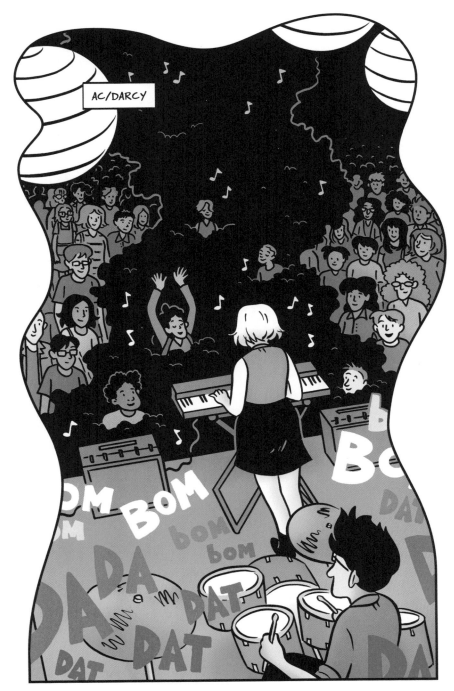

bom
bom
DA
DAT
DA
DA
Yeaaah!
WOOOOOO!
A/C DARCYYy!
That's our set!
Anne Surly's up next, followed by our **secret headliner.** Who's excited?!
YAAAAAA!

AC/DARCY, reporting for door duty! You're off the hook.

How'd it go, Darcy?

We crushed!

Good luck!

Thanks!

Thank yoooo-urp!

Luck? Don't need it!

GREEN ROOM

Hey, Kesi? Got a paper bag?

Don't need one. I'm not stressed at all!

ZIIIP

We already played our worst show ever. We've got nowhere to go but up.

dab

fluff

I wasn't asking for you, I was asking for—

Lora? Are you gonna make it through the show?

I . . . I think I burped it all out. I feel better, now!

What should we do? It's too late to cancel the show.

She says she's okay. Maybe she's okay!

Hear that? Anne Surly's on!

Anne Surly

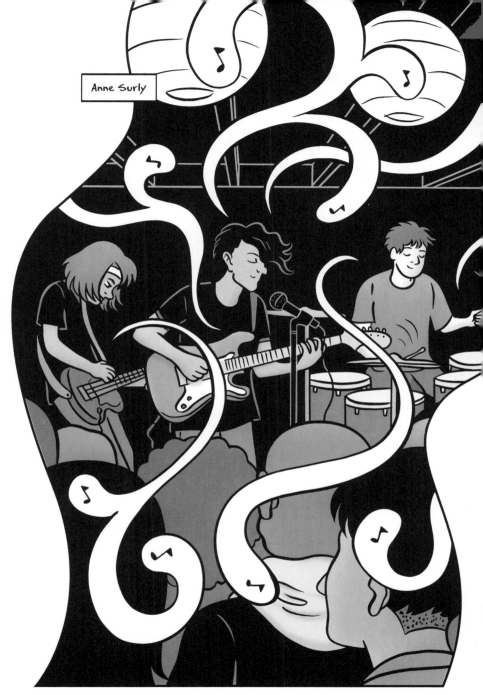

ivu
Thanks so much! We're Anne Surly!
ivu
And now, introducing your "secret" headliner, one of the best new bands in LA: Fancy Pink!
And here they are now!
AAAAAAAA

Thanks, Cooper.

Thanks, Anne Surly.

Thanks, AC/DARCY.

And thank you for being here.
We're Fancy Pink.
WOOOOOOOO!

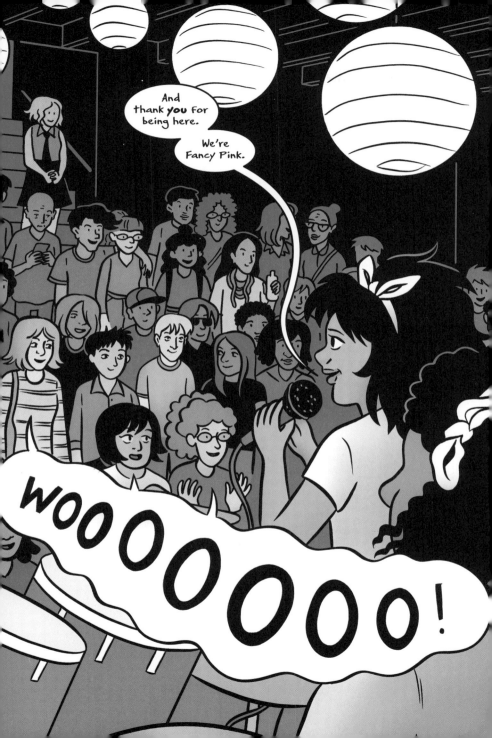

GRAB
BRAAANG
DADA
DADA
DA
DA
dun dun dun
dun
dun du

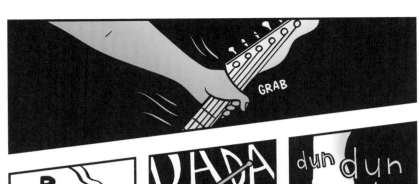

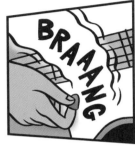

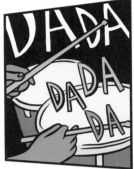

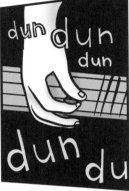

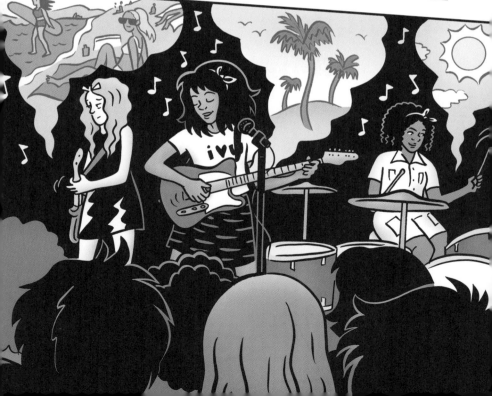

HOLLYWOOD
i♥u
i♥u
I thought playing the Echo would be a dream come true, but this is so much better.

This is where I belong.
WOOOOOOOO!
Thank you!
This next song is for, um . . . for a friend.
They know who they are.
i ♥ u
One, two—
CLACK
CLACK

BELCH
ivu
Three
I'm sorry! I—
URP!
The tacos—
BLARF!
murmur
murmur
whisper
GREEN ROOM
mu
I, uh . . . don't think she's coming back.

BLARF

Um, Charlie?

Can you go hold Lora's hair?

On it!

BLARF

Sorry, everyone. I guess we're just gonna . . .

Stop the show?

Run away?

No! We can do this!

glance

nod

We're gonna play the rest of our set as a two-piece.

jingle jangle

Daisy petals one two three
I'm not keeping score
but I know that you probably are
If I got it wrong you'd know
and call me out in the
back of your big sister's car
We sound okay!
Not great, but . . .
Once you liked me but I messed up
couldn't see what I had when it fell at my feet
I know my timing's off
it just took me a while
to hear my own heart beat
dun
duh
dun duh
dun
duh
Huh?

Cooper!
He plays bass?!
duh dun
BRAAANG
dun
duh
DA
Wink
dun
dun
dun
DA
DA
I like you, I like you not
I like you, I like you not
I like you, like, a lot
Can I have another shot
Can I have another shot

April, May, June is here again
Are you sticking around
do you have somewhere to be
Want you to meet all my friends
but tonight let's be exclusive
you and me
I like you, I like you not
I like you, I like you not
I like you, like, a lot
Can I have another shot
Can I have another shot
Another shot
ping

W
It wasn't supposed to go like this—

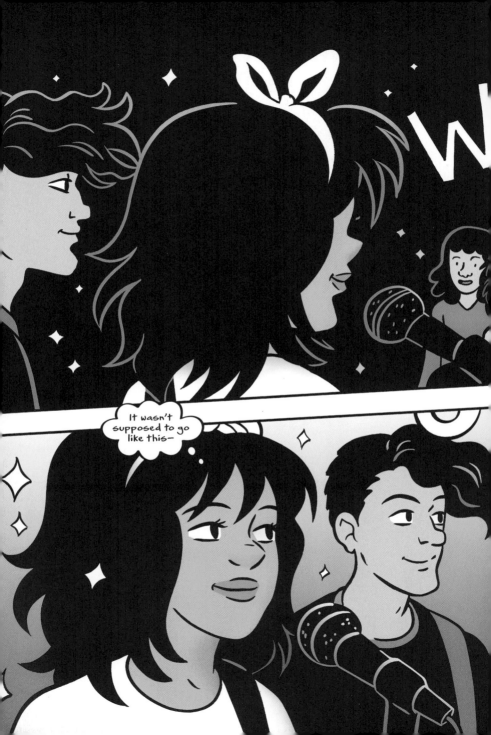

SOB!
That's my new favorite song, and I might never hear it again!
Shhhh. I recorded it on my phone.
but I wouldn't change anything.

After the show

Hey.

Austin!

Um, I—

What now? I spent all that time thinking about making the grand gesture.

I never thought about what comes after.

I like the new song.

Really? But—

But you said you only came 'cause Charlie said you should.

Come on. When have I ever listened to Charlie?
I came because I wanted to.
baDUMbaDUMbaDU
Ahem.

Lora! Feeling better?
Yeah! For real this time.
Sucks that I missed the show, but guess what?
What?
We did it!
Really?! We got the money?
ivu
WE'RE MAKING A RECORD!

Um—I told Charlie I'd meet her outside, so—
Oh!
TAP
I'll walk you out.
Aw
hee-hee

So—bright—

It feels like it should be dark.

Like when you go to a matinee movie, and when you come out—

OhmyGod!

Mom? Dad?

Mom?

What are you doing here?!

We wanted to hear you play!

But how— how did you hear about the show?

I told them.

Charlie! You ratted Bina out?!

I did not!

Kids! Enough!

Give me a little credit, huh? It's my **job** to know when cool new bands are breaking.

Bina wallpapered the east side with Flyers For a tantilizing secret show, but there aren't any secrets in this town. The folks who run Sinkhole are old Friends of mine.

Those Flyers worked a little too well, I guess.

So, um . . .

What'd you think of our set?

Granted, we were listening from out here, but . . .

You sounded great!

We're proud of you, Bee.

I'm not in trouble?

HA HA HA HA HA

Oh, you're in huge trouble.

You'll have to hold off recording your album, because you're very, very grounded.

You're grounded?!

You didn't tell our parents, right?

i ♥ u

We-e-e-e-ll . . .

HONK HONK

185

KESI!
Get your butt over here!
HONK HONK HONK
Crap.
Lora!
Grab your stuff. We're going!
We were so close to pulling this off.
Hey, we got the money.
And an album title!
Album title?
What are you talking about?
Come on! It's obvious.

Three months later, somewhere in Eagle Rock

Fancy Pink
GROUNDED
LIKE YOU NOT

Daisy petals one, two, three

This is the best song ever.

Maybe we should start a band.

Yeah.

Definitely.

Meanwhile, a few blocks away

The End